A Possum's Nest

Written and illustrated by Toni Hough

To Dear Frances,
    Love & hugs from your Australian family.
                                    The Harrises

Please keep my pages intact.

Lily stepped onto the verandah as sunlight broke the dawn.

She looked across the garden at a baby possum on the lawn.

She lifted him up gently and held him to her chest.
He had lost his mummy and was in much need of a rest.
She thought she'd better try to help him find his home.
She could not leave him here, frightened and alone.

Past the old rope swing to the path between the trees,

Lily found a tiny nest, disguised within the leaves.

"Is this your nest?" she asked, looking at the tiny babe.

"I don't think it is but be patient and be brave."

"This nest is neat and cosy
and very sheltered too.
This nest belongs to ROBIN.
It's far too small for you."

Lily walked a little further, then something caught her eye.

It was a nest of grass and twigs with shiny things inside.

"Is this your nest?" she asked, looking at the tiny babe.

"I don't think it is but be patient and be brave."

"This nest is very pretty with
all its decorating.
This nest belongs to MAGPIE
who's always celebrating."

Lily wandered deeper into a dappled, dense woodland.

There above the treetops, a nest so very grand.

"Is this your nest?" she asked, looking at the tiny babe.

"I don't think it is but be patient and be brave.

This nest is surely large enough, it has a wonderful view.

This nest belongs to EAGLE

and is much too high for you."

Lily was feeling tired, her legs were getting sore.

Where she sat down to rest, she saw a nest of leaves and straw.

"Is this your nest?" she asked, looking at the tiny babe.

"I don't think it is but be patient and be brave."

"This nest is soft and warm,
nestled in the ground.
This nest belongs to BANDICOOT
who doesn't make a sound."

Lily stopped to listen, she thought she heard a bee.

To her surprise, a man-made nest hung high up in the tree.

"Is this your nest?" she asked, looking at the tiny babe.

"I don't think it is but be patient and be brave."

"This nest was specially made,
when tree hollows can't be found.
This nest belongs to ROSELLAS,
the prettiest pair around."

Along the cleared bush track Lily slowly made her way.
There above her head was a nest of mud and clay.

"Is this your nest?" she asked, looking at the tiny babe.
"I don't think it is but be patient and be brave."

"This nest is strong and sturdy
and was surely built to last.
This nest belongs to MUDLARK,
I think we'll just go past."

The little baby
possum woke
with a
rumbling tummy.

He was feeling
very hungry
and really missed
his mummy.

Lily had looked in all the places she thought his mummy might be.

She found herself back home beneath the peppermint tree.

Just as she was thinking the baby possum would have to stay,

a gentle hissing above revealed a nest that's called a drey.

Soft grunting from the possum nest
beckoned the baby back inside.
Where he quickly joined his mother
and snuggled down to hide.

"This is your nest" said Lily, looking at the tiny babe.
"You were so patient and also very brave.
Your nest is safe and warm, you're back with Mum again.
I'm glad we found your nest, goodbye my special friend."

This book is dedicated to my children Josh, Lily, Jai and Riley - Toni Hough

WILD
EYED™
PRESS

First Published in Australia by Wild Eyed Press, 2013
Reprinted 2020
Wild Eyed Press, 33 Warren Road, Nannup WA 6275
wildeyedpress.com.au

Text copyright © Toni Hough 2013
Illustration copyright © Toni Hough 2013

Cover and layout design by Simon Blackburn

Written, illustrated and designed in Australia.
Printed in Australia.

A823.4
ISBN 978-0-9875054-0-8

More books by Wild Eyed Press

WILLIAM THE WILD - Leanne White

WILLIAM THE WILD GOES CAMPING - Leanne White

HE'S MY DAD - Leanne White

SHE'S MY MUM - Leanne White

MERINDAH AND LUCKY - Leanne White

DILLY DALLY ALL DAY LONG - Leanne White

AN ALL AUSTRALIAN ALPHABET BOOK - Leanne White